MATTHUE ROTH   ROHAN DANIEL EASON

THE
GOBBLINGS

THE GOBBLINGS

For Iris, for your patience.
— Rohan Daniel Eason

b"h
— Matthue Roth

The Gobblings

Copyright text © 2015 Matthue Roth
Copyright pictures © 2015 Rohan Daniel Eason

ISBN 13: 978-1-935548-60-7

First published hardcover edition by One Peace Books, Inc. in 2015

1 2 3 4 5 6 7 8 9 10

Cover and Interior Design by Richard Rodriguez
Edited by Robert McGuire

One Peace Books
43-32 22nd Street #204 Long Island City, NY 11101 USA
www.onepeacebooks.com

Printed in Korea

Herbie didn't like his new house
very much at all.

It was far off in space,
and all of Herbie's friends
lived several
star systems away.

The nights were long and cold,
and outside every window
was the same boring expanse of stars.

5

The minute they landed,
Herbie's parents
were rushing around,
building this machine and that....

...and so there was
nothing much
for Herbie to do

except play with his marbles
in the corners
and on the stairs.

6

This gave Herbie a chance
to notice the little things
in the space station,
the things that nobody else
ever paid attention to...

...like the tunnels
that ran throughout
the walls of the station.

But inside the walls,
there were other creatures
who also went unnoticed
by the adults
of the station.

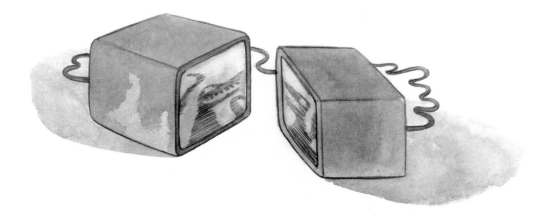

"Herbie, please stop playing with the machines,"
his father said to him.
"Can't you just go
and keep yourself occupied?"

So Herbie tried
to keep himself occupied.
He looked around the workshop
for something to do.

Herbie's father sent him off
to the landing deck
with a pile of gears.
"Why don't you try to
make something with these?"
he said.

So Herbie went off
with his pile of gears.
He found a spot
on the landing dock
that was sort of private

and tried to
keep himself occupied.

He built himself
some robot friends.

But Herbie didn't realize
that the gobblings
were keeping themselves occupied, too.
They were occupied with
watching him.

Before Herbie and his parents arrived,
their space ship
picked up some visitors.

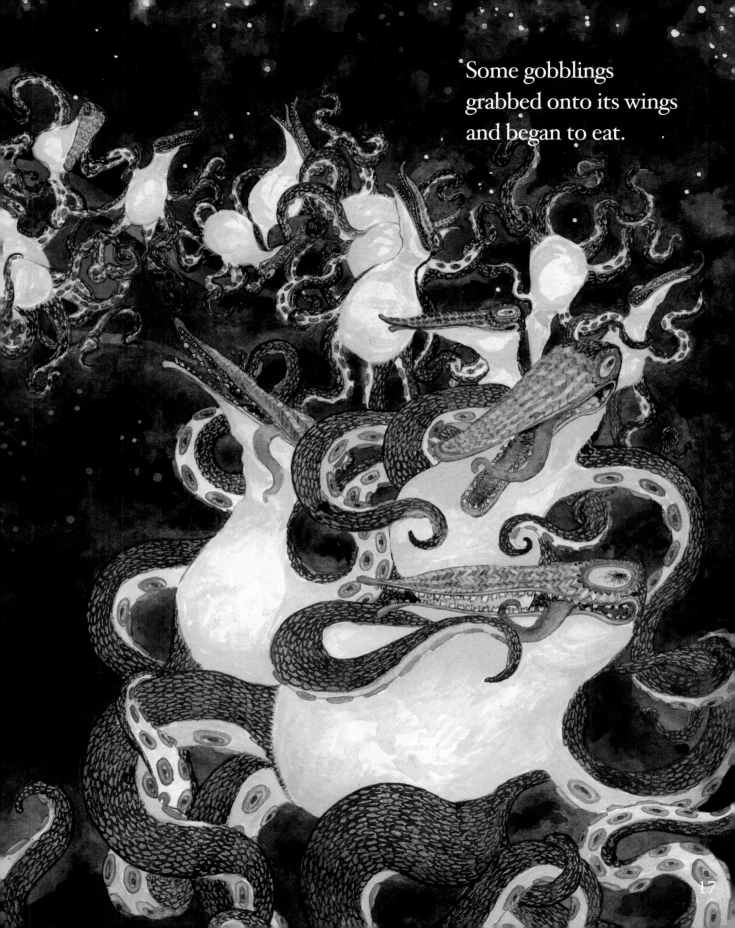

Some gobblings
grabbed onto its wings
and began to eat.

17

The gobblings were space pests.
They were like ants or mosquitoes.
Instead of sipping blood
or eating candy, though,
the gobblings liked to munch on metal.

Sometimes they feasted on old moon mines.
Sometimes they ate space trash,
or parts of old ships.

18

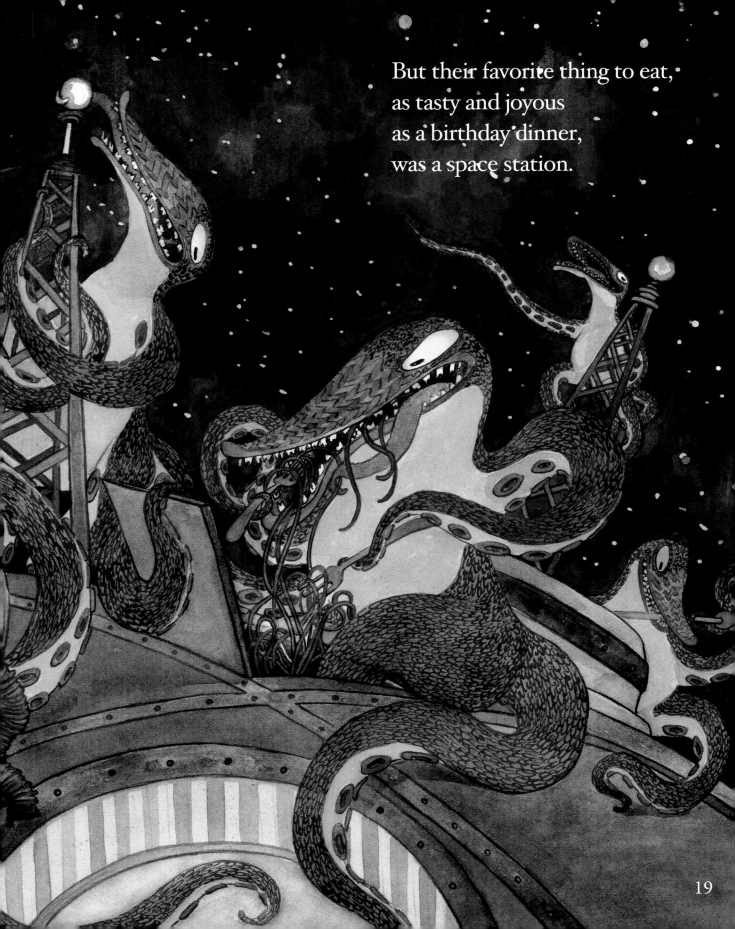

But their favorite thing to eat,
as tasty and joyous
as a birthday dinner,
was a space station.

19

While Herbie and his parents unpacked,
the gobblings scurried away.

They found the spaces inside walls
and they found the machines
that made the space station run.

The machines made power
so the space station could fly.

They made food
so people could eat.

They made air
so people could breathe.

All these machines were like candy
to the gobblings.

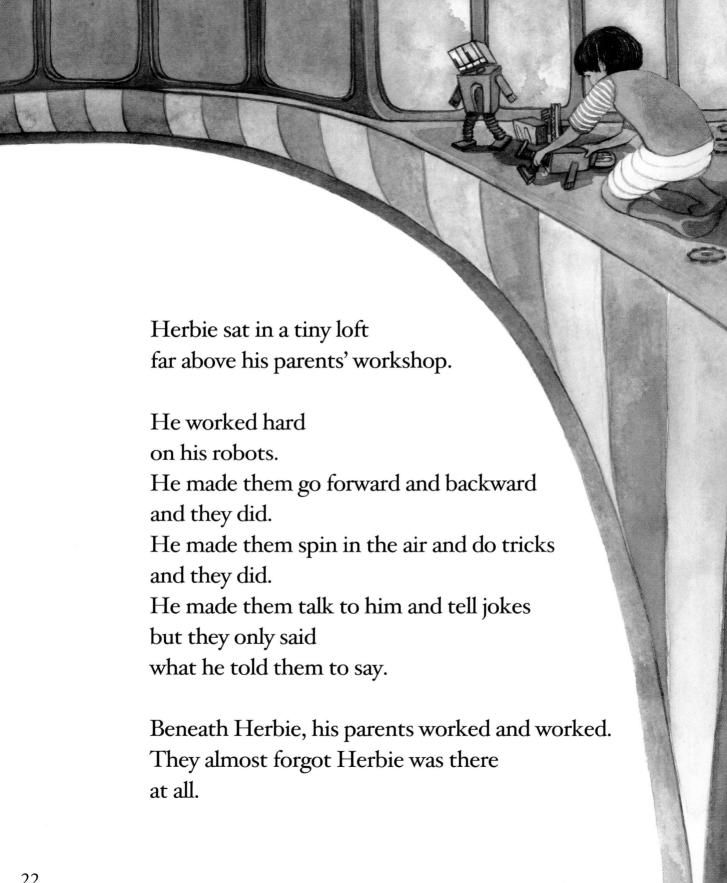

Herbie sat in a tiny loft
far above his parents' workshop.

He worked hard
on his robots.
He made them go forward and backward
and they did.
He made them spin in the air and do tricks
and they did.
He made them talk to him and tell jokes
but they only said
what he told them to say.

Beneath Herbie, his parents worked and worked.
They almost forgot Herbie was there
at all.

Suddenly, the lights went out.
"Mom?" Herbie called down.
"What did you guys
do now?"

But Herbie's mother and father
were speechless.

The gobblings had eaten
every last machine.

The only machines left
on the whole space station
were inside his parents' workshop

and the gobblings
were trying to break in.

Inside one gobbling's mouth
was the lever that kept the landing dock closed
and kept them all
from flying into space.

Another held the button
that kept the station moving forward.

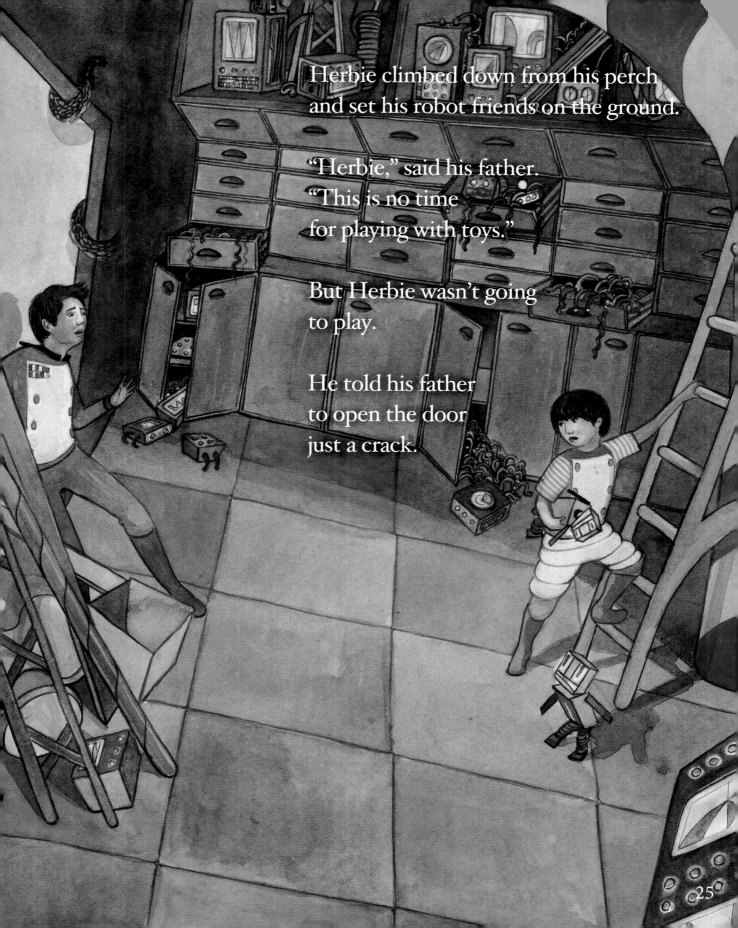

Herbie climbed down from his perch
and set his robot friends on the ground.

"Herbie," said his father.
"This is no time
for playing with toys."

But Herbie wasn't going
to play.

He told his father
to open the door
just a crack.

Herbie waved one of his robots
through the crack
in the door.

("Mmmmm," said the gobblings,
licking their lips
when they saw it.)

Then he jumped through that crack,
himself
and he ran.

Herbie raced down the hall,
two of his robot friends
tucked beneath each arm.

The gobblings scurried
fast behind.
Nothing was yummier to them
than a tender, juicy robot.

In no time at all,
Herbie led them
to the landing dock.

He tossed one robot
at the gobblings.
One gobbling caught the robot
in his mouth.
He chewed and chewed.

"Yummmm," he said.

The others crept forward to see.

The gobblings feasted
on his robots.

Herbie jumped into the closest ship
and slammed the door.
He pressed the button
to open the loading gates.

The winds of space
rushed in.

The gobblings flew off the ground
and out of the station,
tumbling into the
eternal night.

29

Herbie was shaking.
He felt good about himself,
but he also felt sad.

He heard the people on the space station
cheering.

His robot friends were gone,
and he didn't have
any other friends
in the whole star system.

But he would make new friends,
one way or another.
He was good at making friends.
He knew that now.

Herbie's parents
ran to the landing bay,
scooped him up
and gave him hugs and kisses

even though Herbie didn't really like
hugs and kisses.

"You saved us," said Herbie's father.
"One day, maybe you'll run
a space station of your own."

31

"Maybe one day," Herbie said.
"Right now,
I'd rather just
explore."